Miss Bindergarten Celebrates the 100th DAY

of Kindergarten

by **JOSEPH SLATE**

illustrated by **ASHLEY WOLFF**

PUFFIN BOOKS

"Tomorrow we celebrate," says Miss Bindergarten,
"the 100th day of kindergarten."

"100 days of friends, 100 days of fun,
100 days of darling, dazzling, winning work you've done.
So remember that tomorrow all of you must bring
100 of some wonderful, one-hundred-full thing!"

That night—

Adam's fort is finished.

Brenda's
half asleep.

Christopher's
one hundred blocks
tumble in a heap.

**Miss Bindergarten gets ready
for the 100th day of kindergarten.**

The next morning—

Danny counts out cereal.

Emily fills a vase.

Franny draws a picture of her hundred-year-old face.

Miss Bindergarten gets ready

for the 100th day of kindergarten.

Gwen creates
a poster.

Henry claps
and cheers.

for the 100th day of kindergarten.

Gwen creates
a poster.

Henry claps
and cheers.

Ian brings a relative
who's lived a hundred years.

Miss Bindergarten gets ready for the 100th day of kindergarten.

Jessie pokes her polka dots.

Kiki carries tarts.

Lenny hugs
a bagful of
a hundred
candy hearts.

**Miss Bindergarten gets ready
for the 100th day of kindergarten.**

I COULD EAT 100 PIZZAS TOMMY

I COULD EAT 100 CRACKERS KIKI

I COULD EAT 100 BANANAS gwen

I COULD EAT 100 GRAPES URSULA

I COULD EAT 100 ICE CREAM CONES CHRISTOPHER

I COULD EAT 100 PICKLES Ian

Ophelia's stuck with stickers from her hat down to her boots.

Miss Bindergarten gets ready

for the 100th day of kindergarten.

Patricia sorts her crayons.

Quentin revs toy cars.

Raffie lifts the lid up on one hundred dinosaurs.

Miss Bindergarten is *almost* ready for the 100th day of kindergarten.

Sara checks her ant farm.

Tommy flies his kite.

Ursula's bag is heavy, but **V**icki's bunch is light.

Now Miss Bindergarten is all ready

for the 100th day of kindergarten.

Wanda whoops and hollers.

Xavier shakes his seeds.

Yolanda Pound and
Zachary Blair
boogie with their beads.

"Congratulations, kindergarten,"
says Miss Bindergarten.

"Without more delay...

let's celebrate the 100th day!"

HEAVENLY 100 DAY HASH
Pick 10 pieces from each bowl: cereal-os, pretzels, marshmallows, nuts, sunflower seeds, raisins, choco chips, banana chips, cereal pillows, popcorn.

Adam's Fort
100 Popsicle sticks

Brenda's Chain
100 paper links

Christopher's Towers
100 plastic blocks

Gwen's Poster
prints of 100 fingers and toes

Henry's Sweater
100 buttons

Ian's Relative
100 years old

Jessie's Clothes
100 polka dots

Ophelia's Decorations
100 stickers

Patricia's Box
100 crayons

Quentin's Bag
100 toy cars

Raffie's Box
100 dinosaurs

LET'S CELEBRATE THE 100TH DAY!

Miss B's Dress
100 bows

Wanda's Lariat
100 rubber bands

Xavier's Packets
CORN PUMPKINS BEANS MELON
100 seeds

For Mickey, Mikey, Mark, Anna Maureen, and Annalea —J.S.

For Judy and Gerry, teachers and friends —A.W.

Our appreciation to Lynn Taylor, who introduced the celebration of 100 days in kindergarten in the 1981-82 Newsletter of the Center for Innovation in Education. Mrs. Taylor recently celebrated her 25th anniversary of teaching in primary grades in California and New Jersey. She was influenced by the late Mary Baratta-Lorton, whose theories on teaching children number concepts and math have been widely adopted. Mrs. Baratta-Lorton was director of early-childhood education at the California Center.—J.S. and A.W.

PUFFIN BOOKS
Published by the Penguin Group
Penguin Putnam Books for Young Readers,
345 Hudson Street, New York, New York 10014, U.S.A.
Penguin Books Ltd, 80 Strand, London WC2R ORL, England
Penguin Books Australia Ltd, 250 Camberwell Road, Camberwell, Victoria 3124, Australia
Penguin Books Canada Ltd, 10 Alcorn Avenue, Toronto, Ontario, Canada M4V 3B2
Penguin Books (N.Z.) Ltd, 182-190 Wairau Road, Auckland 10, New Zealand

Penguin Books Ltd, Registered Offices: Harmondsworth, Middlesex, England

First published in the United States of America by Dutton Children's Books,
a division of Penguin Putnam Books for Young Readers, 1998
Published by Puffin Books, a division of Penguin Putnam Books for Young Readers, 2003

20 19 18 17 16 15

Text copyright © Joseph Slate, 1998
Illustrations copyright © Ashley Wolff, 1998
All rights reserved

CIP Data is available.

Puffin Books ISBN 0-14-250005-4

Manufactured in China